God,
The Maker Of The Bed,
And The Painter

Mark Nepo

God,
The Maker Of The Bed,
And The Painter

LC# 87–81730

ISBN 0-87886-128-9

Ithaca House Books
The Greenfield Review Press
2 Middle Grove Road
Greenfield Center, N.Y. 12833

"Beds, then, are of three kinds:
and there are three artists who superintend them:
God, the maker of the bed, and the painter."

— THE REPUBLIC, BOOK X,
Plato

"Poetry is not like reasoning . . . for the mind in creation
is as a fading coal, which some invisible influence,
like an inconstant wind, awakens
to transitory brightness . . ."

— A DEFENCE OF POETRY,
Shelley

for God,
the maker of the bed,
and especially,
the painter

and for Anne,
her spirit braids the three.

ACKNOWLEDGMENTS

Acknowledgment is made to the following publications for poems that originally appeared in them:

University of Windsor Review: "Of Nightjars And Songbirds," "Sunup"

Manhattan Poetry Review: "The Engraver"

Colorado-North Review: "The Lost Petal," "The Helmsman Lured From His Post," "Crimson," "Takaski," "Beyond The Ring Of Seawine," "The Circumference Of A Pledge," "First Snow"

Greenfield Review: "Mountain Berries"

En Passant: "The Rusted Pail"

New Mexico Humanities Review: "Skittish," "Richard's Panama"

Chariton Review: "At A Standstill"

Poetry Wales: "Meleagrina," "God, The Maker Of The Bed, And The Painter"

Boulevard: "Zila And The River"

Croton Review: "Night Of Comets"

Washout Review: "Libretto For A Garden"

Kite: "Owls Prey On Mice"

"White Rage," "Young Carlyle And Sloane," and "The Rusted Pail" were included in the anthology *North Country*, published by The Greenfield Review Press.

The cover is an engraving by M.C. Escher, *The Rind*, © M.C. Escher c/o Cordon Art—Baarn—Holland.

God, The Maker Of The Bed, And The Painter

IV. MELEAGRINA

V. THE ENGRAVER

VI. GOD, THE MAKER OF THE BED, AND THE PAINTER

I. THE LOST PETAL

THE LOST PETAL

(for Tu Fu, 712-770)

I

In August at a bend in the river, a flower edges out,
its root in stone and the brush shakes a braid of light
across its stem.

There curls, on the quiet flower, a petal which collects
the gold-dust babbled by men before they fall.

I reach, and in my naked charm,
each thoughtful woman's muscle,
each gentle man's skin.

Old voices surround the lighted stem
and I tremble as if too frail for the wind.

II

Against my fingers the quiet petal shreds
and as I bend to drop what's left in water, I am certain
another does the same, a continent away, and when we rise,
another two will reach, will tremble, to dip their shredded
parts, and then, two more till the Godly gesture skips
the way a rush of air shakes the leaves about a bird,
and startled, he flies

                    looking for food along the river
where he spots a worm or twig bobbing near the bank.
He swoops and nips and flies.

And like a small mind with a large idea,
he shakes his beak and drops the half-chewed petal
which breaks apart between mind and grass.

3

III

In March at a bend in the path,
the old mountain flower nods
and I am cold,
afraid to root my feet in stone,
to spread my arms to unknown Gods.

Old secrets burn in a mouthful
if the eye can weave
the leaf to the star.

Spirits surface.
My numb lips swell.

IV

The poem remains, a hybrid of gold-dust
and the best of explanations
when love prompts a translation.

So much emerges from the life within. Like the beaver,
we protect ourselves with what we gather

and all the scaffolds we can conjure
crumble when the heart sees out there
a sky, a face, a stone or wrinkled rose
that it has held within.

BELIAL'S COMB

When strong, I do not understand why the great did not
accomplish more. But today, I can barely lift my eyes.
It is easier not to stir.

Here, I trace the molding,
the worn spots in the rug, all the while looking
to myself, a passage I read over and over,
never keeping my thoughts to the page.
The sun through the curtains drapes half my face.
The dark side feels empty.

I am glass-eyed and useless,
beyond the dreams which move soft men,
beyond the dark winds which entice old explorers.

I have lost the urge.
My edge seems aflame,
but I feel no heat, feel nothing being consumed.

The ideas have become machinery and my head purrs
against the sunlit pillow. I want you to stay with me today,
to listen, but I've nothing to say, and by noon,
I will inch back into myself, the stubborn turtle
whose temper is gone

                    like every mind ignored while alive,
thought curious when dead, forgotten for a while,
then allowed to rest.

Why did Leonardo surround himself with idiots.
A genius bears only brilliant flaws.
I love your father's barn, though I've never said so.
The barn cats squint in the door's light
like lepers in a cave. And your father calls
the trough, a manger.

I'm afraid to have a son, afraid
I'll love him more than my poetry, afraid I'll not be
who I think I am.

It was only last month I felt
Michelangelo in my hands, sweeping firm strokes,
never hesitating, never questioning.

I have done nothing
but look at my hands since.

I am frightened today
that you will find me ordinary, retying my laces,
tripping on the stoop.

THE CIRCUMFERENCE OF A PLEDGE

Jack is eight with eyes that are twenty.
Gina's five, delighted the count is still on one hand,
and Kevin plans to quit smoking.

It was important to move the bed,
no need to sleep in a pit of memory;
so the vacant studio is where he wakes
and their bedroom is a fresh museum.

As the smoke ascends, he thinks out
what custody really means;
feels for unwritten stories and new themes.

The urge toward the typewriter waits
vertical in its case and Kevin
stumbles about, puffing back the ceiling,
circling the hard shell.

Jack doesn't want to shower
and Gina grabs the last two cigarettes
from the table, squealing:
"You promised! You promised!"

And the man puffs himself alone.

He remembers before the marriage
an apartment in New York
with a moody Puerto Rican.

He remembers the keys and their
pat-pat--pad-da-dat-dat
against the stiff bond;
the bell, the carriage,
lost in the momentum of the story
and she, hot-blooded, waiting for more,

wanting the machine silenced;
the story spinning itself, her voice far off.

She put a lighter to the page.
The carriage blazed a thin yellow.
The hot blood danced.
He slapped her down—

"You promised! You promised!"
Kevin steps from the rings of smoke:
"Just one last one, honey."

Jack bounds in, face clean, neck dirty
and Kevin sends him back to the sink.
The boy whines and the man teases and pokes
till the eight year-old swings blind arms
at daddy.

He wheezes
and Kevin butts the cigarette
and holds his son.

"I didn't think mommy would go.
  Where did she go?"
And the man rocks his boy.

The sheets of fear unwind like a downpour
late in winter. Trembling fingers scan the table
for one more cigarette, but Gina plays on the floor
with broken sticks of tobacco, singing:
"You promised! You promised!"

OWLS PREY ON MICE

Two large men like cats scrapping
scratching, splitting lips: who knows why.

I slow as others form a circle.
I thought someone would stop them,
but the faces are expressionless, relaxed.
I hear a jaw pop like wood dropped on ice
and blood spots the cement.

I watch the stain spread, unable to leave,
and catch my face in the store window, expressionless.

A siren, a blue and white, a flurry of close noises
like hens chased about a coop, and they are gone,
and the crowd without touching each other, ambles on,
blood drying on the sidewalk.

When fifteen, I was fisted unexpectedly,
could see the cold knuckles approach.
I staggered, then felt the burn on my chin.

The bastard smiled and walked away.
His leather jacket rustled down the street.
I stood breathing hard, the cold air all over
my split skin. He was drunk.

Younger still, an Italian boy, leg back, went to knee me
when my mother interfered. The boy stopped, I went for him.
He sneered and pumped his leg when my mother interfered
and took me inside.

When the bully cornered me on our backstoop,
my father, stern, locked the screendoor.
I thought he didn't love me.

Several times while away at school,
my mother wrote how he cried that day;
so much did he want me to be a man.

The blood has dried anonymous and mine,
and I feel weak, afraid of silhouettes.
How easy it would be to live as the antelope,
knowing the leopard is the one with the spots.

FIRST SNOW

In the car, on the way, she started to sing.
It drew me. I took her hand and she stopped.

Later, the three of us took iced roads
to cut a douglas fir, and on the way back,
I traced the route for the year he dies
when it will seem so important for us
to find our way.

After dinner,
he talked of how the salmon
are drawn upstream
by a magnetic pull
in the earth
and someone spoke
of the caribou in Alaska
forging the same river each winter,
and how building a dam deepened the river
and they are drowning by the hundreds:
sleek leathered bodies rolling the shore,
antlers breaking like boughs.

After cake and tea, we went to sleep
and before dawn, a yelping.
He was up scrambling for his gun,
sockless in boots and out to the sheep.

Down in the brush behind the barn
a coydog was steering a deer.
He hollered and threw stones.
Growling and white dust.
He fired into the snow
between them.

The coydog vanished. And the deer,
in the moon, stunned in the snow,

11

stared out like any son or ingrate
or child of God given another chance.
As if being saved were its right,
it leapt the blue crust.

WHITE RAGE

The children, knee-high, are splashing in the lake
despite the abnormal quiet. The pines seem to stiffen,
the wind circling in a voiceless gasp. My dog, a setter,
at the water's edge, barks at the children's laughter,
his gold chain bouncing light about his neck.

My mother-in-law, barefoot, with a tray of sandwiches
heads for the dock. My wife in a sweatshirt reads in the shade.
The functions merely cycle: food, laughter, solitude. Is it
wrong that I feel closer to the pine and birch. I understand
the high branch, resilient, holding as the trunk creaks
and sways.

Clouds roll in.
There is a privileged glance of the others
without the glare. The squirrels have stopped, sidelong,
gray fur breathing in and out. There are no birds,
and now the lake is flat, the children
looking up, puzzled, arms dripping, hearts racing.
Only the dog continues, up and down the bank,
half-jumping, half-pacing.
                                        A pink sheet cracks

        I'm snapped from my feet
                                                long wood breaks

            my wife rolls the ground

                                        the whack of branches fails

her mother thrown flat   the birch drops slowly
for her legs.
                            I try to push off, to rise, to run
but cannot move, my skin hard. A spotted fire crackles,
the split birch steaming in the rain. I try to roll.
The dock has planks afloat, the children out of view.
The rain is fierce, the lake muddled. Mother

is pinned as men in boots run to her.
My face cools. A stranger steadies me.

My wife strokes my face, "I was afraid to touch you.
You were so still, and mama's hurt. I can't stop
shaking."

Slate from the cabin's roof covers the bank.
Some jut in the soil like thin slabs
of loss.

The children huddle inside,
the tops of their huge eyes pressed to the window.
Men swarm about the smoking log and now,
wet smells and dark skies will bring us more fear.

Nothing matters as the white veins flash
in the distance.

My setter lies in the water asleep,
his metal chain sizzling, his legs
bobbing in the rain.

I wade to my knees and float him to shore,
as if dirt were safer than water,
and the thunder fades, dancing to the crack
of a white and gaming whip.

YOUNG CARLYLE AND SLOANE

You understand Bill Sloane died Thursday
and the ground's hard, Mrs. Mckee, it's goin' on Thanksgivin'
and the ground's hard like a fist in ice,
all gnarled and battered.
They wanna hold him till the thaw.
But I won't have it, I tell you.
Bill Sloane was a good man
and I won't let his bones wait till Spring.
The tombstone man — he's greedy with his time —
wants all winter to carve 'rest in peace.'
He's Carlyle's boy, a liar if there ever was and his old man —
worse than a hot day in December,
make you relax and then snap, cold as hell.
No, by Jesus, I had no use for Carlyle.
I wouldn't spit in his throat if his stomach were on fire.
The ground's hard, Mrs. Mckee, but Sloane was a good man.
I'll need a pick-axe and a spade
and the sweat'll dry as fast as it comes.
You understand it's right to dig a grave for a good man
and downright sickly to make way for a liar.
When Carlyle died, I had to dig all mornin' in the rain.
He had a solid brass box, solid brass and the mud weighed
as much as the brass. My legs ain't been right since.
I dug all mornin' and don't you know, Mrs. Mckee,
young Carlyle showed and started talking down to me
about some digger in Yurick. By Jesus, I'm no educated man
but I know the difference between a liar and a good man.
And Sloane was a good man, warm till the day he died.
Carlyle was a brain, cold like a fist in ice,
like the ground, Mrs. Mckee.
I never told no one, but two years ago in June,
the moon was bright. I dug my own, you understand
and put boards across. I thought I'd dig my own, you see
I'll be no burden and you needn't plant flowers —
just swear the box'll be made square.
The dirt's in my garden. But the boards have rotted

15

and spiders and coon and possum and snakes
keep buildin' nests and draggin' straw
and bark, keep makin' home.
You understand, you can't keep the life out.
You understand, there is no rest.
The life above is gone and the life below can't wait.
There's no rest, by Jesus, and young Carlyle won't have all winter
'cause Sloane won't hold till Spring.
It's cloudin' up. I've let the sun slip again
and the ground's gonna be stubborn as your head.
You understand, the grave don't dig itself.

TO LIVE OUT THE GIFT

(for Grandma)

In the sun, in the yard
between the brick towers
where orderlies eat hardrolls
and yawn; in the sun
with her rubber brake on
and her footplates heating;
in the sun, for the first time
in seven months, she beams back
to the fresh earth she has not yet forgotten.

In the sun, in the yard
of the facility, she says,
the warm breeze brushing her face,
"I want to go home."
I wheel her around.
She says the trees are beautiful,
the clouds are beautiful.
She says the pansies and stray
wounded hungry cats
are beautiful.
She thinks the dirty bricks
are beautiful
as she inhales the light
and sighs, "Why can't I go home?"

Her white hair is swept in a wave
and she is healing in the sun,
and I start to feel
we are home.

She closes her eyes
and the heat is laced with bees
and the warmth and buzz drape
her strong near-century lids

17

and she smiles, then looks beyond the garden
and says, with a laugh, "Where are we?"

I start to retrace the day,
to frame her in, but the sun
like a knell of God overwhelms us,
and I rub the wind from her face.

She takes my hand, washing it
in the dish of air between us,
and says, serenely,
"I don't know where we are."
And I confess,
all organs of memory
in my throat,
"Neither do I."

MY CONSTANT DREAM

Some are born to yes
and some to no.

Still, each has one spot
without trace or print
from which the rest
blossoms like a storm

and if you feel almost in love,
if you wait for some kiss
to put the future in your eyes,

if you relive your cuts
like an iron to a crease,
tell me, please:

how come the cost of love
lingers, a smoke that films the mind?

I fear, if not used up, our hearts
will dry in our bodies, like oceanless fish
breaded in the sand.

RESTLESS IN THE CLEARING

(for George)

You twist and burn a lineament with me that no one sees.
And if you were to ask, I'd spend a long day with you
and near the end, when the dark was as brilliant as the day,
I'd say, "The sky between you and your greatness
is the white hood in your mind that keeps
the lineament hidden."

I don't have that kind of courage.
But in Plato's way, it's where
the perfection of the thing
really lives.

I, in more ways than most, play Zorro
with the dreams of those I love.
But you, you wear your mask of truths
like facets of a prism.

THE HELMSMAN LURED FROM HIS POST

I

The stemmed glass waits on the captain's shelf
for that ritual which affirms: ours is the one,
full with life's secrets and forgiving.
But there seems no peace to victory,
only more refined loss, linens
to hold the sulking head lopped off.

Lives acquiesce to what they do best,
soil becoming mud becoming fertile,
snow to stream to rivermouth to sea.

The quiet ones create, rediscovering
what others have seen but thought unimportant.
The shadowed see only the color of their guilt,
every Judas born looking for his tree.

II

The shoremen unhitch the thick sagging ropes
and step with ease about the slick morning docks.
The old mate watches the young buck struggle with a winch
and wonders how much to leave him on his own.

The beggar shows his son how to work the pier
and in the darker seas of heat, a tribal mother struts,
her tray upon her head till her little other struts,
till tradition struts the ocean miles.
It ripples us. We are its wave.

Our porous hells drift clouded water,
swirl a little further, and settle
noiseless in the sand.

III

If meant to be agile at the helm,
nothing will happen to your hands, unless
you flaunt your gifts.

If destined to be a great general
who will drop his shield into the Nile, unable to resist
the Queen's red and flexing breast, nothing will prevent it.

If fated to see and then go blind,
the stupor will be ours, for what is most crucial
you will witness: too much is as crippling as too little.

IV

The quiet ones witness the wind's fingers in the sand
and each takes the gesture as his divine omen.

I will offer you my questions,
if you will ask them elsewhere.

Must I write them down?
The wind blows and the port lights flicker.

BEYOND THE RING OF SEAWINE

You say I look through you, intense and somewhere else,
that you're being strangled, not in the usual way,
but as if when I enter the room, I inflate
till the corners are all you have.

You say my madness is my clarity
and my mad eye ticks,
my wild voice gruff.

You say I need to see from where you are
and you are right—the womb of your eyes,
the calmest blue my life has known.

Some say the Amazon is longer than the Nile.
We will go sometime to the Peruvian spring
from which it flows. We will go and bathe our arms
in the shoals the Incas call Apuŕimac.
We will lie in the mouth of the Great Speaker
and come away, glistened members
of a large and speechless truth.

I want your head on my chest, as always, on my chest
where I soak up your ideas as you sleep.
They seep till the knot inside my heart slips
and underneath gels a calmer heart, and finally,
I sleep.

If the air we ride makes us numb,
prick the damn thing. We can start anew.
We are most loving when fragile and unsure,
most daring when just about to fly,
lost chicks breathing hard, tossed from the storm.

THE MYSTICAL LOVERS

They argued and laughed. She went to rebut.
He swept himself into a buck and vaulted off.
She stretched into a crow, slick as light.

She tired and preened on a wet bough.
He circled, grazing beneath the tree.

She fluttered higher and the buck became a hawk,
lifting through the limbs. They squabbled from branch
to branch and then he knew. The crow was just a crow.

He hovered the field, pumping just enough
to stay aloft. He'd lost. He landed, himself,
and walked the stream.

He kicked the water, ankle-high
and sat along the bank. The brook tailed off
and dropped. The drop emptied into falls.

The sun broke the clouds and he lay on his back,
now a small log, riding the falls.

He crashed and swirled the rocks,
floating in the shallows. Driftwood
on a warm day was best.

He rolled across some lily pads, spun sideways,
tangled, then turned himself to peel his arms free.
In the wet stems, she appeared, laughing.

He reached for her. She turned a cat and scrambled for shore.
He splashed and chased, a labrador. She turned a pup.
He licked her neck. They played about the shallows.

He became himself and held her to him.
She turned a bobcat, fighting him off.

He turned a leopard and pulled her close.
She turned a lion, all looks and paws.

He turned a woman much like her.
She turned a man.

They turned themselves, all eyes and flesh
and tumbled in the lilies.

SUNUP

Waking, my leg across your back, tangled in sheets.
I remember dozing, the window open, the covers off.

That we writhe in sleep is proof
of the muted ballet, the inner life.

You stretch, and wind the tangle tighter,
rolling your hair into my breath.

We shift like cats, all day in the sun.
Your stockings sway on the curtain rod.
The scent of alyssum drifts through them.

TABLEAU IN MAGENTA

On days when the rain clears early
I like to try new restaurants alone;
watching elbows rock small linened tables,
all with real flowers, singular in water.

You were slouching, legs crossed,
drink in your hand, staring off.

The way you held the glass,
fingertips firm, made me believe
you were a painter.

You posed the kind of fantasy
I seldom want to trust.

You were so at ease with yourself
that when you scanned my waiting eye,
you did not look away, but took my color
as part of your own imaginative heart,
smiling to yourself, how lovely
the soft thoughts of this garden.

Your dark hair was rich,
your complexion healthy and I knew
you were the better dreamer. As for me,
my stomach growls at five
whether in love or not.

I even felt the invitation
in your mind, saffron on the edge
of an inquiring eye.

In the time I took to consider
if you wanted kids or kept a neat bed
you were looking elsewhere, swirling your drink.

Years ago, I would have made a go of it,
but delicious is this distance
which leaves your cheek in the sun,
a lady slipper safe from my touch
and ruin.

LIBRETTO FOR A GARDEN

(for Robert)

There is only the same eye fixed on the same winter branch
and those moments flush till he feels the movement of thinkers
now long dead. He believes they see him
picking at white twigs in the silver brush.

In such a mood the nearest voice becomes silk
and the snow misting his face is an occasion to weep.
In the hush, he hears the earth
as the branches lean in careful mime.

There are others behind his eyes,
others blind in their own time.

The wetness spreads across his lip
and the spindled birch dips, blessing the unseen
about the garden. There is no urge in him to record it all.
It is enough, somehow, to let the wind
shape him like a crooked branch.

Like an icicle beneath a fresh sun,
his mind unfolds, one clear drop
reglazing all.

MOUNTAIN BERRIES

I was stopped by Tu Fu just below the tree line.
He was wandering from the snow-still peak,
his white hair heavy, and I went to tell him of his fame,
to ask him how to keep the will strong.

He took me to the east of the path, pointing across the range,
"Did you come along the Yangtze. My wife waits
below the mist. Have you come through Honan. . ."

His voice was wispy and as he spoke, he walked
through mounds of stone and chest-high boughs,
"Or have you come from Witch Gorge. I have friends there, too."

I reached to steady him, but he walked through my arm,
"My daughters were dressed in patches the last time.
They thought my hair too white, and cried
when I couldn't lift them. Will you read their poems
along the mountain so my wife will know we are near."

He stepped into my body, slightly taller,
and I felt his breath inside my own, and I was Tu Fu
who wrote his last poem staring at a plank,
slouched near death in a boat on Lake Tung-t'ing
half-way home, to my wife, my children,
half-way from the Witch Mountain fireflies
to the clustered chrysanthemums, across paddy paths
to my thatched house in Honan.

A chill swept from my neck to my teeth
forcing me to cough, and he slipped from my mouth
sighing, "Your eyes search your mind
and you are ashamed not to know, not
to discern Honan from Szechwan. . ."

I felt he had no right.
He stopped my thought.

"You must strain to see how the water slaps
the moorings, how the gibbons groom and cry and nest,
or if they nest first, but if you can't see
what you're looking for, see what's there.
It is enough."

His wrinkled eyes went wide,
"My daughters think I'm dead.
We must hurry."

His long arms started down the mountain,
"Come, the peak will always summon, but this descent
from wild air to mountain berries is saddening."

We wandered and in the next clearing,
he showed me a sliver of furled light
on the edge of lake below.

We kept on and as dusk came, he said,
"The rippled clay beneath the sun and water
gives hope to those
who shape themselves to others."

II. KELP-ASH

ST. JOSEPH'S ORATORIE, 1934

Brother Andre had them rub oil
from St. Joseph's lamp as a sign of faith.
His wall was covered with braces and wooden feet,
with crutches and split canes.

She'd come from Quebec, deaf and powerless to speak.
She'd been taught the stories: a man crippled by his brother
rose stunned and walking, a festered child left well.

She was the driver's side hit by a bus
and for days a fever scorched her focused eyes.
Her skull roared and she sank cold, near blue,
chilled to the scalp. For three nights she shivered.
Her mother prayed against a coma while she froze,
a macquette of ice in the fresh white bed.

She woke to mother's smile mouthing short words.
She went to leave and nurses appeared out of her silence.
She yelped until they raced their lips and held her down,
poking needles while they chattered.

Mother had died in June
and now she'd come alone, had prayed to St. Joseph,
and the first thing he gave her was the oil.

She was afraid to rub it in.
He smiled and poured the oil on his hands.
He rubbed her ears. It made her cloudy.
He wiped some more behind her lobes.

He coated her lips. She wiped it off.
He checked her arms, and opening her jaw,
he rubbed her gums. Oil numbed her tongue.

She felt like a cheetah, cornered by jittery men,
all poking spears. She swiped the spear to her right,

felt a jab from behind. She swiped and spun, claws
dizzy in the heat. She pounced and broke the circle.

She ran in a smooth relentless gait
over brush which did not snap, on past giraffes
chewing in the muggy trees. She stopped, drowsy,
panting in the jungle. A sudden flash through a branch.
She crouched and hissed, then pranced a mile or so
and found a clearing near a hidden falls.

She curled and panted, head pounding,
the sound of the falls, a marvelous thunder
rising in the mist. The heat of the grass
and roar of water over rock
made her splash the edge and wade.
The falls grew louder. Her fur matted smooth.

She waded further and the gurgle of her breathing
squiggled as she sank in water so fast and cold,
the bottoms of her eyes
began to shudder.

                  She wriggled for the surface,
but lost the use of her limbs as she pumped her head,
a sea lion, leaning, surging
through the muffled dark.

                  She heard bubbles escape her mouth,
heard water shiver past her ears as she surfaced beneath ice,
nose raw against the underside, sniffing bitter air
and down again. Her pelt felt thick
as she dove.

                  Above, a crevice of light
broken by quick and slippery forms. The crevice widened
and warmth filtered down. She pumped her neck up, up
to where a hunter's hand grabbed behind her ear.
She heard his fingers slap against her skin.
She honked and whined, fighting the air.

He lifted the girl's face
and she opened her eyes, waiting.

He leaned and whispered, "St. Joseph did not forget."

She rose with that stunned miraculous look
and hugged the old man whose shoulders were cold.

He refilled his lamp with oil
and tacked the girl's kerchief
to his wall.

ZILA AND THE RIVER

Zila stole seascapes by dawn
before Pharoah's daughter could call.
She shuffled through the sea grass
which bordered the river. She made the wet blades
obedient. And if she looked long enough,
the grass would move and not the water,
like groggy bitterns all in a line,
all necks dipped forward.

Zila held her robe about her thighs, wading
to the north. A small ark bobbed in mid-river.
She watched it slow and spin and tangle in the grass.
It was tightly woven, a thatch of papyrus. It caught
and spun, and she lifted her robe above her waist, slipping
deeper. The water felt cool against her belly,
soft past her sinking hips.

She tipped the near corner. It was covered with pitch
and dark at the seams, smeared with bitumen.
On a nest of reeds within, a naked babe, still,
half-wet, eyes wide and unalarmed.

Zila let her robe spread below the water
and dropped her hands into her floating lap.

She felt the grass wash and wrap against her legs
and reached for its roots, her ear submerged as she yanked.
She heard the grass pull free, muffled,
as her breath slapped the surface.

She set the clump of reed beside the babe
and started for shore.

She hid the boy along the river
and returned to the palace,
trailing water from her legs.

Zila was certain, the child
was a gift from the river.

She went to Rhemus, a guard who was a sometime lover.
He laughed and listened and longed to have her damp limbs
wrapped about him.

She avoided Pharoah's chamber, took a pouch of grain,
a sac of milk, two towels and a robe.

The boy cried as she dried
and bunched him in the oversized cloth.
She mashed the grain and mixed the milk,
but the infant could not chew.

She held the child and he quieted some.
She nudged his small lips about her breast
and the little one began working his tongue.
She could hear the slight clicking and feel her nipple
rub against his palate.

Her breast grew sore.
She'd find a way or give the sea
its babe wrapped in pitch.

She smuggled the boy into her small chamber
and late on what became a starless night,
the Pharoah's daughter, informed by Rhemus,
pulled Zila's sheet and took the boy.

She wept for nights, the clump of reed
beside her pillow.

II

When the boy was grown and forced to flee to Madian
for killing a guard, Zila followed to the edge of the river
where she walked, troubled, pulling at her oldest shore,
floating one stalk of the grass she'd saved.

As her muscular legs began to sag, Zila was dismissed
from Pharoah's chamber and she married Rhemus
whom she never forgave, and they had a boy.

Rhemus was rough with him. He kept pushing his fingers
about a spear, but Zila would bring him to the river
and let him wade.

Rhemus brought him into the guard and Zila
let another stalk drift out to sea.

When the torrid voice prophesied, white-haired and mad-eyed,
stammering before Pharoah, his heavy staff full with plague,
Zila knew it was her babe wrapped in pitch. For days,
she kept to herself, avoiding Rhemus, wanting to take her boy,
to touch his staff, to hear the strange God in his mouth.

The weeks which passed were dreadful, infested
with gnats and flies and locust. Rhemus, on a hot night,
blamed Zila for not drowning the madman in the river.

It was late and starless and all of Egypt began spitting blood.
Rhemus dressed for war and their little boy curled
into a red cough, a red wheeze, a thin shiver which rippled cold.

She ran to the street, saw horses shriek and collapse,
saw women clawing at their fevered husbands.
The air began to smell. She tried to stir
her boy. He unfolded and fell,
a moist and rabid ghost.

Rhemus blamed her and left coughing.
Zila picked up a knife and dropped it, shoved a chair

and backed away. She broke the reeds she'd yanked
below his ark. She snapped them all and flung the ragged grass
at her foaming son, damning the river and Pharoah,
the strange prophet and his God. She tore her robe
and wept herself groggy at the foot of the dead.

When she woke, she found the stems
like merciless angels,
intact and fresh beside her head.

KELP-ASH

A thousand feet below, bubbles seep and ascend
through the iced black waters
as the earth trickles and breathes,
regular and rising.

The newborn across the globe have slate-colored eyes
which turn blue, turn brown, turn speckled green,
a sign that each has received its soul.

We rise and squirm in the earth's affection,
never sure how we ascend, and man, the upright one,
migrates in lusters, fastening iron and word
to everything stronger.

Minoan slaves were paid with olives
as if fruit could sweeten a man in chains,
and that which outruns the fastening animal
becomes its deity and its prey.

The Northern lights flourish as Dvořák's *World* subsides
and the silver-haired matron locks up the mailroom
now that all her friends have retired. She wonders
why the years roll aside like a harpsichord-glissando,
why the points of light, once caught, flash through aging palms.

An eager Armstrong wipes his trumpet lips as Marvell's
green thought fills a green shade, and the same slow smile
appears; the same singular rhythm of the large crow
whose wingtips curl in one upturned pump
off the snow-crusted elm.

The envied ones see through the wood,
knowing as the farmer separates his bales on Sunday,
the next Degas determines if the blue just spilled
is useable, and both love the detail
of a handled tool poking about.

And somewhere, Rembrandt taps his brush,
delegating background to those hungry for a part
while he pulls at the light, shifting the source.

And father and son utter flaws and treaties,
swirling their beer in some long-avoided bar
after mama's died; too fragile to touch,
too aimless to go their ways.

And Galileo checks the Cardinal's eyes
before speaking the universe:
what good truth in a casket?

And Wolsey, obese and dying, rolls his head
to the rainy sill, knowing at last that courage
starts in the stomach
with a whisper.

And here, Lawrence and Kierkegaard are stopped
as my uncle taps his pipe, recalling the chimney fire
when he was a boy, the roar which sent everyone running
but his father who dumped a pound of baking soda
like dusted sequins atop the flames.

I keep my finger by the paragraph while he tells
of the pale olive walls, after scrubbing the smoke
and washing the stains, how he argued with his father
not to repaint the kitchen olive, how chimneys and sudden starts
have always been olive, how his sternest memories of father
have turned pale and olive.

Watching the bare branch sway behind the brook
while Mrs. McNurty speaks the neighbor's divorce,
I chart the landscape with the stranger's lips;
waiting to record it all, later, when the talk seems full
like a Sunday meal and Mrs. M reties her apron
with a glint and a nod.

I watch my mother run the net across the dirty tank,
sifting and letting go, till what's left settles
and the fish pucker and wriggle again.

I watch her rinse the net,
knowing this is how I treat my mind,
how Lowell wrote poems.

And I am jealous of Plato for the myth of Atlantis,
searching for a worthy jewel to fall from my head
and blossom like a waterless rose
when someone in earnest
stares deep into its chance.

If I can't leave Hegel long enough
to notice the neighbor doesn't walk his dog as much,
that when he goes, he tucks his scarf way up high,
complaining he's always cold; if I can't read his poor blood
and the tragic spirit as one,
it falls apart.

How ironic to call natives who gather sponges primitive.
The young man's dreams are the old man's skies.
The oldest occupation merges horses and hawks
as if no one ever dreamt of Pegasus.

I struggle and struggle till like a diver
tangled in his hose, I surface with the brilliant algae,
crimson and soft as pumice; satisfied for the moment,
as the colors fade once brought to air.

III. NIGHT OF COMETS

TAKASKI

*"I want the right of what is called life,
of the leopard at the spring,
of the seed splitting open,
I want the right of the first man."*

-Nazim Hikmet

We talk of history and precedent,
but where did you learn the shallow breath.
You are the nudged cub; your den the point of vertigo.

And I, I am the wounded hawk atop the leafless tree,
swaying, loving the wind as long as I believe I can fly.

It is not enough to see wind through red maple.
I want to flutter open, to *be* the wind. If I dizzy and slip,
find me, and tuck a leaf behind each bluing ear.

It is not enough to brood you are alone,
melancholy, motoring your Sundays to the sea.
Even elephants stagger toward others.
Even lions share the feast.

There is no measure of fullness but to feel full.
The wheat is breaking apart. Come and be still
or go away!

Your open ear is useless
if you must stare off each time I moan.
Decode it all if you must, but I will not
drop my tears in your beaker.

Life is not a distillation
or a tendon stretched and pinned.
I see no contract or ritual beyond the large cat
licking his paw; no sacred dance

save the way we circle each other
late in spring.

What makes you want to doze,
sunglasses high, tonic in hand,
with my mind, the open book
across your knee.

I yearn to lift your face,
to see you squint, your light hair
mixing with wind.

I want the right to run barefoot
through whatever I can survive;
the right to sleep naked, unfettered by sirens;
the right to dream alone, if only for a moment,
and the joys of you and the world, again and again,
when I wake.

WINGLESS

—for Roger who collapsed, at twenty,
from the pressure of an aneurism
on the front of his brain.

Roger gnaws his finger
staring into the metal rail
clouded by his breath

while the wind strips the orchard,
strewing blossoms along the road.

I rub my hand across his face, his ear,
his neck, his back and he quivers
and the little machine with its amber graph
skips and beeps.

How we wait the Judas-hand
to pinch the blossom that is free,
and as we fall, we think
we should have known.

The nurse tries to insert a pill.
His lips tense as unknown hands
from beyond this darkness
pry at his jaw.

A thin stick is slipped between his teeth.
His jaw snaps it in half,
and I keep saying who I am
and what I do.

Roger looks like a stunned beast. The eyes sag
and somewhere inside this awkward mountain,
Roger pounds and careens, wanting out,
wanting to glare at me, to hold his head,
to freeze the blossoms
before they perish.

It's no use, Roger,
I marked them on the way
and as I touched, they suffered
the way you curl and wilt,
my hand in your hair.

I say I'll be back, say everything
will be alright, then leave, wanting to taste
the salt in the ocean, eager
to have the weeds grow wild behind the house,
to give everything stubborn enough
not to die, its way.

AS A ROOT

(for Kitty and Monique)

On her back,
legs swimming the red air,
she slips a string
where birth might be
and pulls.

We smoke and sink
to stay light enough
to see Monique as waterfall,
as heat like beauty
washes down her hips.

She sets like summer red,
about to splinter,
to take the sky between her legs,
to move everything in waves,
to dance in hot skin
since it drapes muscle so well.

All of Sodom pours
through her split
and parting softness.

She rides our looks
as Godiva would her stallion.

Kitty mounts the air
and breathes long
on the old man's neck,
and we're no better,
wetting our lips
and spilling our drinks.

And while we eat them
with our eyes, I fear

they are truly free,
unashamed at last.

We're steamed as muts in spring.

I settle in the red walls
and the tongued night of drink.
With Kitty on my lap,
I feel a warmth
I must have known
before I lived in clothes.

I want to praise them
as I would the neighbor's wife
who works her yard and sweats
in all the right places,
tender as a root.

We leave hot enough
to hold each other,
to melt the codes
of a thousand years.

The cold night stings.
We touch the earth.

Nothing is said.
We talk and laugh
and push radio buttons,
have another drink,
and simmer.

I hug each of them,
up close,
belly to belly,
and we part.

The house is dark
and filled with red strings
which tense wet, then open. I strip

to move in waves. I shift
and turn, spin and stretch,
then stir in bed
and pull at myself,
amazed at how I've lost
the heated grace.

NIGHT OF COMETS

I had a story or two, sitting for hours, stooped over the ice,
lines crusted, fish silhouettes below our feet,
slim and noiseless—but everyone, skewed with drink,
went on and on, and I slammed my glass, losing the name
and face of it, as if it never happened.

They stammered and rubbed their gloves.
I railed and threw the bait into the stove.
The sheriff's son said we were out of bourbon.
The others arfed and donned their caps.

They said they'd be back, the way dreams promise a man
he will light again. Man. The animal of promise:
lure, hunt, fire promise with a bow.

This mining town as we broke through was full
of unshaved boys who shift in packs
the way wintered deer yard-out
on the south of the mountain
where the snow never crusts,
where they circle and feed
off berries till spring.
They think in packs
and salivate.

They said they'd be back.
But waiting's for another life.

I hate this clouded interior, need their desecrations
like a worm needs a hook. What's that? Everytime I turn,
the branches lose more snow. I can't stay here.

The night—as I trudge on—the soft coal night
drags through my mind, its hawsehole; creaking,
rubbing raw the lip of all I see.

Again the voices tail off
and the roads wind down to one.

Friends are hard to keep
when the stories burst aflame.

The mine shaft bays and shadows like promise
skip the grass from the moon. I keep looking
for that which never ends.

They say, now and then, a coal vein catches fire
underground, and feeds itself, sometimes for years,
a comet purging the skull of the mountain.

THE RUSTED PAIL

We scuff the high dark grass
to fill the pail for the dying ram
too old to walk or bray.

The flashlights ring his saddened head and folded knee
with broken halos that neither hasten the end nor heal.

And we make sure there is no thirst
in his passing, a wish your father invokes
as much for him as for the sheep.

I go to finger the dying fleece.
But you say no and leave the ram
to the darkening crickets, and we stop
to hear him lick the pail.

I sneak back while you and your father sleep.
The horns feel brittle as he sulks up at me,
belly shuddering in weak rhythms.
I beg him to run the brook and die with the light.
He stares, glass-eyed, heavy beneath his crusty horns,
and I lift, palms thick and deep through his knotted wool.

He does not fight or tense.
He only wants to drink and shudder beneath his flickering star
and I think of a thousand names to name his fall—
not one is him, not one is me,
not one the quiet white below his shedding chin.

He is heavy, too heavy. We fail
and the matted grass beside the pail
springs slowly up, while the grass beneath us now
grows warm and waits.

SPIKES AND CLUSTERS

I press my lips to your neck
and beyond, I smell your scent
and keep my breath to your skin

knowing in whose eye we huddle
the deepest are honed to this,
a naked embrace, against the torrents
of street talk and silent ache, a huddle
collapsing in the wildness of grass.

I feel more than I can manage,
a sweetbriar in love with the lily,
the willow's spur falling south of the willow
and all the poems can never catch
your moan beneath me.

Joy rises, a pistil which
surprises despair, the stalk
of awareness. How easily our songs
root in soil where they belong.

We wait the cricket dawn
and horizon fans itself in view.
The still waters move and we must
dress in the light.

My lips frame the wisdom of your pores
which when you're gone
spills from my mouth: a laugh,
a cough, a fiber of word.

AT THE THOUGHT OF A HOMELAND

They say you're not anchored
and I say O yes
like a bird to the wind
and they say but a bird has a nest
and I don't know what to say
except that I love you.

They say you are self-centered
glorious with mirrors
and I say it's his infatuation
with reflection
and they say
Narcissus
was an old prisoner.

They say you are tangled,
floundering in love
and I think of you crying
in a London flat
by the butane stove
at the thought of a homeland
other than in our hearts.

I think of you
bringing me to a bluff
above the river
where you wanted
the beak of the hawk
to skim the belly of Heaven
and you reared as it approached.
Good God, you slapped my back
when it disappeared.

I think of you
as a hidden seam of light.

They say you are a disappointment
and I say some are born
to move like truth.

OF NIGHTJARS AND SONGBIRDS

Your mother's dearest friend now waits
for her burning lids to slip.

She was always the first to note the goldfinch in fall,
her windows braided with feeders and posts.

They found a nest of tumors
which tripled for the air it took to see
and her longtime oracle tossed his wire rims
across his desk, rubbed his filmy eyes
and murmured of days or weeks but
said nothing of autumn.

How I want to hold you close
as if her death means a storm is coming
or worse, just tomorrow.

We can't seem to sleep
so we busy our heads
with things we've neglected
to water and plant.

Finally we call and interrupt the silence
with quivered phrases till she speaks like a needle,
having shed the useless embarrassments.

She has signed the long avoided papers
and now must put her house in order, and if time allows,
she'll stock her feeders and watch for the whippoorwills,
fast-stepping at dawn.

GLOVED TRAINER TO THE FALCON

The far edge of the angel's sword
burned bronze then silver
and the oak was forever in spring,
attended by buds.

The tree had its own source of light,
hushed and golden. Her sword
had touched nothing in many thoughts
and she hovered there, an impaired belief.
The grass was matted with fallen fruit
which did not spoil.

                    A crow cocked near.

The sword flamed high.

"C'mon, let's eat, let's know."

The bronze scorched silver.

"I'll fetch for you."

Her sword swiped blue.

"Here, put your mouth to this.
I'll wake you if God should be about."

The angel watched the light brush slick
along the crow's chest
and she landed. Her feet wobbly,
not used to the ground.

She tossed her sword which crackled,
but the grass did not burn,
and she worked the fruit,
her mouth juiced and core-filled.

She stretched beneath the lowest bough
and thought, poor Eve. She writhed and felt her legs
press against the Earth. Her wings ached and the crow
pecked, curious, about her sizzling sword.

How marvelous God's tree.
She watched the crow strut through the grass.
How she wished he were a man
and the crow became a man
walking toward her.

He mounted her,
brushing her thighs apart,
pushing back her wings,
white feathers in his fist.

She dropped to his pull,
neck bare, eager for his lips.
He arrived like lava and smothered her.
She broke to gasp. He tugged her wings
and covered her mouth. She broke for air—gagged
in the steam of his breath. He bit her lip
as the branches sagged, then cracked.

She reached—palm through the grass—for her sword.
But he—in satin robes—jerked her down,
gloved trainer to the falcon.

He swiped the sparking bronze
and spiked it near a root.

The birds all turned to crows.
The crows to ravens.

The fire split the ground,
crackling for the tree, and the satin trainer
broke into flames. His finger lit her wings
and, having won his destiny,
he let her flutter as they all became
the appointed blue, the infinite fringe
of a clear and conquering flame.

THE GYPSY AND THE OLD MAID

There was a week of heat,
air thick as honey,
when the flowering crab lost its petals
and the rains lashed the ground
into a chill.

Both barefoot and sweaty
were caught in the storm.

They ran beyond the yard,
clothes heavy and clinging.

She swung against a punky elm.
It cracked. They tumbled
and wiped mud along the other
till they rocked wetly in the soil.

After, the birds trilled and chirped
and the brush seemed a jungle.

Their mother found them near the stream.
He was on fire. She was ashiver.

Doc Stephens said it was a fever,
but the boy kept burning, a tic in his eye,
while she quivered, ice about her lids.

They both lost weight
and the virus passed.

The summer ended,
her eyes lost interest,
his complexion darkened.

When old enough, he left home
with a sharp tongue and a beard

looking for motorcycle women
and doors with broken screens.

She stayed on and seldom went out,
just sat by the porch watching starlings swoop,
listening to the rain spill from the eaves,
sporadically, like unintelligible secrets
babbled by a God.

THE FISHERMAN

The boy wants to learn but the old man
will not let him even come aboard,
for the boy still thinks wisdom
a matter of tongues.

The old man goes only for the globefish.
The risk has made him delicate,
a master after hours of bladework.

The boy fishes elsewhere, catches a shark
and leaves it near the old man's boat.

The master buries it when it begins to smell,
unimpressed.

The trick is not to cut the spline.
The old man recalls a broken son offering his catch.
The mother froze numb, then one by one,
stiff and tumbling; bodies found clean and healthy,
simply not alive.

Legend has it the Devil bred a pool of fish
fed by his ill and patient hand till at the flood,
he stroked Ham's face, and Ham, unnerved,
brought both on board the Ark.

The old man has seen much,
drifting in the schools of dories,
their prophetic lines bobbing taut to slack.
It's not unusual to watch a young fisherman
gleefully slit his fish apart.

Lulled by the ease of the catch
and the yellow of the afternoon,
it's not uncommon
that he might think it a skate

and taste it from his knife, to tremble sharply,
his wooden frame careening the ribs of his craft,
for the careless gutting of his globe.

RICHARD'S PANAMA

The Winnebagos rumble out of the horizon
like Jonah's disciples from the mouth of the whale
and the old Spanish man in his leathered skin,
dark and quiet, hears the boards creak
in his little store as horns honk
and dozens of even-teethed gringos
stretch and yawn and slap each other in the dusty sun.

The old man smiles. How funny they look
with their dark glasses and pale knees.
How funny, the gringos with no eyes.

They make fast noise and grab all his batteries
and juice. The women want his light bandanas,
the ones the caballeros buy to fend off the sun
when the old ones tear from sweat,
from too many knots.

The short-haired eyeless men laugh and take
his spam and rope and swarm through every can.

The gringo women brush their hair
and wave his bandanas at him.
His screendoor slaps.

His shelves, barren, show their warp
as he runs his fingers over quarters and dimes
which pepper his counter like buckshot.

SKITTISH

Something in this life
wants us to drive nails for a living.
Something hounds us to earn money.

I see my wife drop her delicate stare
and rub her tight feet on the edge of the bed.

While she sleeps,
I note the new lines in her brow
and I am sure it is only fair
I buy some tools and look to build for wage.

But what I really mean to say
is that the carpenter is not forced to write poems,
and even rodeos only pay
for the quickness with which
you can tame.

CROSS-EYED AND PURE BRED

Walking the hard ground, still hearing violins
from the car radio, the hazard lights clicking,
I am stopped by the possum three miles back
frozen to the asphalt.

I shake the ice from a roadside pine.
There is barely a scent. I remember the night
a siamese, cross-eyed and pure bred,
back-pedalled from the wheel of a Datsun,
clipped anyway. We were silent while the cat,
uncut, leapt from corner to corner,
pawing the fire in its head. We drove on,
the siamese twitching like a man
burned alive in his knowledge.

The prospect leaves me quietly stripping
the ice sheath from the branch, too aware
of this fragility, merciless and certain

as grandma begrudging Pop's sudden death,
or mother with her bloodless brother
sorting grandma's towels, and me,
staring through the phone, never dialing.

It seems easier to ride the snow with violins,
to stop and twist the frozen branches,
consoling to break something smaller
when so many of us
are heard snapping
in two.

KLEPSUDRA, THE WATER STEALER

—an ancient Greek device that measured time
by marking the regulated flow of water
through a small opening,
such as the mind.

Only the good hours pass quickly.
We should grow in clumps like the trees
by the river where late in march bird wings
flick like crickets against the pine.

Instead, we go our way, growing strong,
fleeced rams whose horns sprout so full
they can't see to either side

and suddenly, at lunch or later,
after a movie, there's a perky one
in a red dress or a group, half-drunk on wine,
laughing, and the breeze teases warm, then gone
and the quiet airs a doubt
till the best memory of touch leads to more
like the mental dancing which breaks free of step
in a thoughtless direction.

The dream slips to illusion
when the eye steals a glance.

STILL TOUCHED WITH FIRE

Given the memory of light,
the blind lover glows,
wanting love to be no more
than honest movement
toward something fleeting.

Fantasies freshen the deep, then disappear
like water poured about a drying root.

Given the space of a lifetime,
why not be foolish
and grope
to be that which pours
or that which roots.

For Lovers move toward,
not away, knowing
without knowing
that the eye arrests nothing
the soul does not entreat.

IV. MELEAGRINA

HELLEBORE, EATEN BY FAWNS

RICHARD:

(She leans to the mirror, slip in hand,
thighs pressed against the sink,
a Degas dancer waiting for a cue.

The moon looms through a wet branch.
She pulls the skin on her brow. Now it will begin.)

ELEANOR:

"We can't go on like this. You come, you go.
I never know where you are.
If someone thinks we're close,
you go off for days, hunting
and hiding in bars."

RICHARD:

(Her hands on her hips, pacing;
her hair, skirting her shoulders.
I have trouble hearing what she says.
Why must anything change. Why can't we talk.
She is open, ready and I fit her perfectly,
a larva stretching in its cocoon.

I love when we don't plan love,
when we drop magazines and tumble,
not caring if the bedspread's mussed,
if our clothes line the floor, not caring.

She is in pain, though I can't make out the words.
She is wincing. But I have nothing to say.)

75

ELEANOR:

"When we touch, you're not there.
When you shave — I doubt if you feel yourself.
And you want *me* quiet, too,
to eat, sleep, hold your head in the morning. . .
you want the strokes without the art. .
Do you hear me? I'm leaving!
Can't you understand?!"

RICHARD:

(She musn't.   I,
    my insides   a netted fish.
    I shiver, wet   tangled   afraid to speak   while
    caught.   Don't leave like this,

    I,   need space   and you, at the perimeter.)

ELEANOR:

"You are entombing!
    Your silence — Venomous!

Beneath that muscle you call a heart, I have seen
your heart. .   But I will heal.
You'll never find another —

Don't you have anything to say?"

RICHARD:

(The moon is caught in the wet branch.
    The feelings splinter. Hold on.

Her unguarded movements look awkward,
fumbling.)

ELEANOR:

"I deserve some words from you.
I've earned the right to touch you
somewhere else than between your legs."

RICHARD:

"I   have trouble hearing what you say
I   need space

You looked beautiful in there,
your thighs pressed to the sink

Why must anything   change   "

(My fingers twist the netting.
I hear the door, in the distance, slam.
The moon moves from the wet branch.)

CRIMSON

I. LANCELOT

"Where both deliberate, the love is slight,
Who ever lov'd, not having lov'd at first sight?"

— *Christopher Marlowe*

Dizzy beyond repair,
my conscience is less
than the wrinkled legging I leave behind,
caution, the hardest focus now.

I wander the courtyards long after she goes,
rubbing my face in her kerchief,
all for the smell of her,
half lilac.

I've lost control.
I follow like the wind a falling leaf, circling in gusts
till atop her and breathless, I am no more.

I press to have it all
before she dresses into Arthur's wife.

Possessed, my lips of coal half fall away,
embers that heat and crumble
against her measured breath.

II. GUINIVERE

"Cupid beats down her prayers with his wings."

—*Christopher Marlowe*

When I hear him latch the door,
I roll away and pretend to sleep
and he sighs, to find me pretending.

He leans against it all, half-veiled,
a creation of my schemes, and through the barest lids
I watch him weep dry tears which shudder
and drop as dust.

How can only this remain:
he feeling safe to cry
while I pretend to rest and dream.

Across this ashen bed, I ache to wake this wooden Arthur,
to wipe the charred lines clean, but he pokes about,
a moping Lazarus, and I can't get past the chill
to kiss the dead.

Yet even last night, below the stars
rolled tight against the castle wall, I dozed and woke,
my legs about poor Lancelot,
his breath sporadic on my neck.
I blurted, "O Arthur, my childlike King."

He whispered, never opening his eyes, "I do not hear it.
I will not recall. I've shed all names
since lying with you, a river across an unknown land.
I am rapid and anonymous with but one course,
to reach the mouth with you."

I prayed that Casseopia might tumble like a dagger,
might strike me dead. I pray for any falling star
to cut the crimson thread I've spun
about these young men's minds.

III. ARTHUR

"It is most true, that eyes are form'd
to serve the inward light..."

— *Sir Philip Sidney*

She still carries all I gave her.
Things I can't do without. Her face,
without my love, is smaller.

Again tonight, I saw them suffer
and hold, eyes seared
like fired jewels.

I'd cut his tongue
and her, those bottomless eyes,
but who would tell me when
I'm wrong, and into what great space
could I stare and forget that I am King.

O Merlin, she teases all but me,
and you have flown. The wind is merely
the wind. What have I done
that I am only Arthur.

I want that day
when through a sea of raucous knights, I saw them struck
by each other. I saw them sweat their love for me
till there was no reason left.

Merlin, find me! How does a man keep his head
when the heart goes to stone, when the breath
tastes of quartz, when the mind dries, a track,
no longer moist, but breakable
as those dead inside drag their stone away.

TOWARDS A MAELSTROM

I

(as a young man)

I take her hand, rubbing her thumb,
approaching a moment I have owned before,
and she shifts closer as I knew she would.

Our spirits were one
in some warmer climb where we both wore less,
both asking nothing, but to walk the hot sand.

Our speech drops away, lost
before the wind can finish, and flushed
we hold, trying to let the blood settle into rain.

I tumble as if falling from Eden
believing her sudden mouth worth any garden,
believing the dark warmth of her hips a cradle
in which I slip naked.

And writhing till I weep,
my rapt spirit comes and flows
as the sun burns the clouds apart,
and then her fire crashes thin.

I watch her dress, the sweep of her arm
through her sleeve, three feathers
on her table.

She hums, still ruffled,
a trace of amber in her eye.

In some other age where I walk a woman,
I am her. She is a flame which works
the illusion of her candle. What she does

81

she does in nothing but those eyes
which repudiate any light they need
like a calm reflecting sea, at dusk,
breaking down the sky.

I sleep on my back and she appears naked,
the loose feathers in her hair. I call her Anada -
then wake to her above me, eyes circling my face,
fingers lightly at my temples.

We think of little but to stroke each other,
hips rolling warm against sore hips.
We reel, a soft organism
grinding out its home.

I am changing in her hands,
glass piping pulled in heat,
my clearness twisting.

I doze and she stretches in the surf, feathers stuck
in her hair, and another woman swims atop her. They laugh,
their bodies slick as they hold back the sea. I chase her
calling   Anada   Anada -

                              She wakes me,
lips moist against my eye.
I tell her we must be married. A week later,
she is gone, a feather clipped
in a pale blue vase.

Everywhere, I see couples parting:
hands dropping hearts like bones
into lakes of no one's choosing.

I wander the river and watch the fat gulls squint
as they ride the chunks of ice too big to drift.

II

(months later)

The hungered soul
sways to unseen drafts.
Appetites work up the flame
and leave it wild.

The more rigorous my thoughts
the less chance she has
the way a flicker cut from air slows
till the flame's curve
dwindles erect and out.

Like a well-guarded secret,
an idea out of focus,
I wane gray,
impervious to heat.

III

(years later)

The outlay of hospitals is a familiar shrine.
Now it seems a ritual to break. My wife and I tussle over habits
and the carriage of a dirty plate. Sometimes I want her to listen
and when she does, I insist there's a world outside what we know.
She seems put sour by the dreams I need to get by.

I search for the glimpse that might spark her
to believe in glimpses.

She frowns, unaware as I what comes from my hand:
what I touch to shock me alive,
what I stir to give it life.

Examining the self is pulling apart a cut.

She tells me her aunt has lost the furrow in her brow,
where she always had that tenacious squint.
She tells me she's glad we went to the hospital today.

I slouch briefly and it is hard
to straighten myself.

IV

(after his wife's death)

I have moved to the shore.
I meet so many people here.
They all return to the sea.
A few yards in the sand, the back of a young woman,
her dark head turned away, and others with their lawn chairs
and coolers. I bring my towel and my books.

The dark woman is shorter than I thought.
She trudges my way. A smile, a nod. She keeps coming.
Beside me, she tips her head and dips her hands
below her hanging hair, fussing with her earrings.
They are unique, she says, sprigs of parsley dipped in gold.
She wouldn't want to lose them. I agree.
Her fingers are slender and soft.

She walks steadily through the surf
with disdain for the cold. The earrings
could be parsley. The sprigs are so irregular.
She lets the surf push her about. It makes more sense
than swimming.

          The sun shoots through the clouds
at random, at me in this moment. Where did I use up my life:
a silly man with a girl's silly earrings
cupped in my palms.

She is dripping and breathing fast.
She sits beside me and uses my towel

and her wet eyes flash familiar, then not.
She stretches and reaches, her body slick.
She is Anada. But she is too short, and too young,
and her eyes are too light. She is Anada. How
can she do this after so many years.

"You are Anada."

She says she is Debra,
but I can call her what I will.
She is Anada.

"Why did you leave without a word?"

She lies so still, denying everything.
She takes her earrings, then my hand
and hopes to see me tomorrow.
She turns her back and trudges away.

The next day I tell her what it was
to find the feather in the vase,
to wonder, to marry, to live
with one who had no secrets.
She says she likes me and what I see
and kisses both my lids.

She says she is Debra, over and over,
Debra, and she's never met one quite
like me. We spend weeks in the water, talking
when no one is about but the gulls and the crabs
and Anada, when she lights behind fair Debra's eyes.

Like a moonraker, I bid her to the dark sand
and in the coil of night, perched above me,
she rubs her fingers along my skull, my life
helpless and open. I beg her to confess,
to set my mind aright. She whispers,
"To name a temper is to tame it."

My mothlike angel flits
from woman to man
to a quiver of light.

Debra looks weary. I take her home.
I ask her to live with me. She is silent too long.
I walk the shore, listening. Again, the surf
sighing like a Goddess, angry and useless.

By the weekend, she is gone, an envelope
taped to her door. I walk for hours,
envelope in hand, my ankles ringed with sand.

There is a note and her twigs of gold.

I toss her earrings to the sea
and watch the sprigs of glitter catch,
and awkwardly, I stoop for them.
They disappear.

MELEAGRINA

(for Anne)

*—along the Persian Gulf between Oman and Qatar
lies the Trucial Coast where, near twenty fathoms down,
the deepest pearl banks in the world rest buried,
and among them, the clearest pearl of all,
the Meleagrina.*

Pearl divers work in pairs, one at the surface
attending the lines and the sinkstone
which carries the other and his baskets
to soft-step the sand for treasures
he hopes he'll recognize.

He walks the bottom,
watching the leaves of vegetation sway
and sways himself till she tugs the cord.
He swallows the little air left
as he ascends.

Aboard, they talk for hours,
placing what was seen,
rubbing the rough
and natural pearl.

In the morning, she dives,
like a Polynesian, without a sinkstone.
She fills their baskets
and he counts the time,
hands wrapped about her line.

They both wonder why the diver like the mollusk
cannot let go the pearl. It seems a matter
of deep embrace, of swaying and tugging
till the mind turns, an open shell.

Descending they can feel the warm current
brush against their bodies. Nothing seems hard
once searching below the surface.

Her slow legs pump as she glides
through sand and coral, and he sways,
his fingers floating, digging in the bank,
knowing this is all they ask of the silent deep:
to dive together as if water were air.

V. THE ENGRAVER

AT A STANDSTILL

I

We were like a herd of frosted deer
frantic for a future, sniffing the crusty path
across the frozen Bay, all for the lovelike chance
hidden deep within the Isle.

And now to wake stranded as the ice returns to sea,
the tongue scratched clean by the scrub pine and the dune.
The love stings, the coldness worth licking.

II

Once I was certain of my version of the sea,
but when the mind cools rippleless,
the calm in Death is the still December wave
flat as ice

and the world could be its own reflection
as the fringes of rise and fall, like frostbite death,
spread and stall.

APOTHEOSIS

*In 1900, Degas bought "The Apotheosis Of Homer" by Ingres
and cut it into some twenty portraits which, once touched up
and framed, he called Studies.*

I will tear this Apotheosis into nothing but heads.
Ingres showed too much, a genius fooled by symmetry,
as if storms are planted in rows.

But the heads, the heads graze some heart-prone abyss.
They smolder, reflexive and magnificent.

The others swirl their cognac and harp on ethics,
but no one owns the source, least of all its trail.

I only know what my eye wants. Only want will work.
Themes are useless. The light falls on a bare cheek,
the cheek moves. The light changes. There is no theme,
only the hint of more, only the magnetism
of the hidden which is ruthless in distilling
from Ingres to me to some artist yet unborn.

Ingres left this mural that I might
stumble through the Louvre this misty autumn day,
half-drunk, half-sullen at what I see
and what remains to be reduced.

These heads implode with dancers' burned expressions
and in another plane, they have legs and hands
in wait, in spin, undressing in maroon light.

My only calling is to change what went before
like the mind that clips the face that paints the gent,
kissing the ballerina as she sniffs his pale orchid.

THE ENGRAVER

(for Mauberly and his Maker)

He worked early, melting the bronze
and once hard, the uncut medallion
seemed a patch of gold ice,
quite calm and possible.

His was to etch the Morpho Menelaus,
the butterfly, the Greek God of dreams.
He had one in glass, poised on a twig.

He caught it years back in Brazil:
quite unexpected, on the edge of the jungle,
a quivering blue, an iridescent leaf
propped on the ground.

He tossed his shirt, all the while hoping
it wouldn't break its wings, tethered in the dark.

Butterflies are quiet fugitives, the Menelaus
and its fan-like wings, mosaics of brown prism
flicking back the blue of the spectrum.
Pilots beaming their nightlights at the Amazon
can see the points of blue flash.

When the Treasury tinted the cruzeiro
with the Morpho's powdered wing, he
tracked one down for ten dollars
and a bottle of scotch.

He had tried twice, but the texture escaped him
and the flawed wing was melted.

Now the shape etched itself.
He polished as he went. He scratched the dream
several times, mixed blue with silver, let it set,
then held it to the butterfly which shimmered.
He stalked his bench. His medallion dull.

He ditched his oils and stormed the Morpho,
raised his stylus like a dagger,
held it like a cross,
and shattered the glass.

He hovered the bench topped with slivers,
fevered like those tropical birds
who nibble the glitter off its wings
and fly away, erratic and poisoned.

He landed and snapped a wing,
grinding it between his fingers,
dropping its filings on his medal,
and as he blew the excess off,
the iridescent prisms
stuck to his thumbs.

VI. GOD, THE MAKER OF THE BED, AND THE PAINTER

GOD, THE MAKER OF THE BED,
AND THE PAINTER

In 1618 at the age of 46, Ben Jonson walked from Darnton, England to Leith, Scotland, some 200 miles, to see his friend, the poet William Drummond. He spent nearly a year with Drummond before returning to England on foot, as he came. Out of Drummond's records of the time comes BEN JONSON'S CONVERSATIONS WITH WILLIAM DRUMMOND, first published in 1711, an extant journal of sorts. *Earlier in his life, at the age of 26, Jonson resolved an argument with the actor Gabriel Spenser by a duel of swords wherein Spenser was slain and Jonson was imprisoned; in fact, enroute to the gallows until released at the behest of a Catholic priest.

*"He recommended to my reading Quintilian(who — he said —
would tell me all the faults of my verse
as if he had lived with me)"*

-William Drummond on Ben Jonson

DRUMMOND:

He left today wearing the same shoes
he came in. What was yet uncalloused was cut
and flapping. His feet were reshaped in bunches.

He is a great lover and praiser of himself.
He promised, if he dies along the way,
to send me his papers,
hewen as they are.

97

JONSON:

My great toe keeps changing as I walk.
Again, the bunions shift. I squint
and there, the blurry specks flare
like Tartars and Turks,
horses and swords
once more.

I told Drummond of my flashes,
of the body spilling its hidden forms.

He scribbled further, stoic
too studious, too good
too simply genuine.

DRUMMOND:

He told me of an epic not yet written. He called it HEROLOGIA.
His eyes went from shelf to shelf in his mind
showing me, forgetting I was there, checking his wares,
and startled to find me across the night room,
he rose and paced:

"The conceit of Donne's 'Transformation' was that he sought
 the soul of that apple which Eva pulled, and thereafter
 made it the soul of a bitch, then of a she-wolf, and
 so of a woman."

I must have stammered, puzzled, queer-look across my face.

He flashed his hands and quickened to a scowl:

"Donne himself will perish, for not being understood."

He dissuaded me from poetry, for she had beggared him,
when he might have been a rich lawyer, physician
or merchant.

JONSON:

Drummond asked several times why I chose to walk.
But Ah- to feel these feet engage the earth, to propel myself,
to rule my own movement, to watch the horizon bob
from side to side when I run—

Drummond's a good listener. He does not balk
at what he does not understand.

When I sit still, I fear I won't get up-
fear my eyes will start to dry,
that the lids, brow and mouth will petrify!

Besides, it's walking that gives rise to poems.
Not strolls, but hikes for days at a time.

DRUMMOND:

He was likeable enough, but he stammered and drifted;
never finishing a thought, as if all sudden ears
to someone not in view, to some lame judge
or changing foe, flagging from his past.

The three of us spent months:
I talking to him, he mumbling to himself;
then arguing with his apparition, just over my shoulder,
wingless and thin.

JONSON:

There are still nights I see that bastard Spenser
falling further on my sword, and then the flurry,
the coated arms bustling me away. There were times
Drummond took his stance, unaware, when lifting wood
or turning sharply if I called.

DRUMMOND:

When he spoke of his dead son, he made me worry;
for the other stories, he buffooned, of his son— he stared off
tightly, eyes lost in his head.

For nights, I found him at the fire
rocking, "Sleep, Sleep, I am forever
fighting Sleep."

I'd wrap his shoulders and sit across the room,
he never knowing I was there.

JONSON:

A man should so deliver himself
to the nature of the subject whereof he speaks. . .
the gray sky rips. . and the stone I lean against is moist
and cold. . . I let the wide ice of stone spread. . and the wind
leeches out the sun. . . O loved boy, it is always
inside dusk I see you grown. .
I am cropped, my festered song gone cold. . .

O loved boy,
how cold these hands, how knotted my chest. . .
a man should so deliver himself. . .

DRUMMOND:

He is somewhere this side of Britain
stopped again by the vision of his boy.
I can hear his breathing on the underside of the wind.
The poor man's eyes are a river bed
and the rough waters now plow their way
churning the sands dissimilar and sad.

He is seized again and mindless
on some Scottish road, anointing every shadow
with the face of his son. . .

                                       my fire's gone out
three times since the sun went down
and only he filled my house
with this peculiar presence.

God spare this Poet, oppressed with fantasy;
he never blocks the source. His world in one step
becomes what he sees. In stride he owns it
and gives it to thee. God spare this Poet
obsessed with a squinting eye, he devours like a storm
and dies when all goes calm.

JONSON:

No stars, always, when I see the clearest −
no stars. But that's not true. They simply seem smaller. . .

It was in Camden I saw him first. . . full grown. . . bloody cross
on his brow. . I woke and prayed to God, to every empty ache
the windless night allowed. .

                              and then. . the letter
from Anne, how he was stuffed with plague. . and then her
bickering, loud even in a dry line.

                          O loved boy. . I hear you
rustle in the brush beyond these Scottish stones. Come
sit with me. Let me wipe the bloodied cross from your face. Come
speak with me. . O Benjamin. . the twigs snap as he runs . .
Their cracks turn gray, then red.

ABOUT THE COVER

The cover is a wood engraving in four colors called *The Rind* carved by Maurits Cornelis Escher in May of 1955 at the age of 57. M.C. Escher (1898–1972), a native of the Netherlands, was an artist of innate, refreshing vision. He brought the seams of various worlds crisply into view. And as music is movement through time and art is movement through space, part of Escher's particular genius was his fascination with time and his want to translate that into his art.

"Man is incapable of imagining that time could ever stop. For us, even if the earth should cease turning on its axis and revolving around the sun, even if there were no longer days and nights, summers and winters, time would continue to flow on eternally . . .

"Deep, deep infinity! Quietness. To dream away from the tensions of daily living; to sail over a calm sea at the prow of a ship, toward a horizon that always recedes; to stare at the passing waves and listen to their monotonous soft murmur; to dream away into unconsciousness . . .

"Anyone who plunges into infinity, in both time and space, further and further without stopping, needs fixed points, mileposts, for otherwise his movement is indistinguishable from standing still. There must be stars past which he shoots, beacons from which he can measure the distance he has traversed. He must divide his universe into distances of a given length, into compartments recurring in an endless series. Each time he passes a borderline between one compartment and the next, his clock ticks."

—APPROACHES TO INFINITY,
M.C. Escher

ABOUT THE AUTHOR

GOD, THE MAKER OF THE BED, AND THE PAINTER, winner of the 1987 Ithaca House Series Competition, is Mark Nepo's first book of poems. His poetry has been published widely in periodicals across the country, in Canada, and abroad. Poems have appeared in ANTAEUS, KENYON REVIEW, MASSACHUSETTS REVIEW, SOUTHERN REVIEW, SEWANEE REVIEW, MALAHAT REVIEW (Canada), POETRY WALES, and 2 PLUS 2 (Switzerland). His work has been anthologized in *THE INTERNATIONAL PORTLAND REVIEW* (1980) which showcased the work of poets from over 30 countries, in the Greenfield Review Press anthology, *NORTH COUNTRY* (1986), and is forthcoming in the Avon anthology, *BLOOD TO REMEMBER: AMERICAN POETS ON THE HOLOCAUST.*

Also an essayist, his prose can be found in *ON LOUIS SIMPSON*, a collection of essays due out from the University of Michigan Press this year. His article, "The Work Of Attention," appeared in the winter 1987 issue of VOICES, the Journal of the American Academy of Psychotherapists.

His poetry was nominated for the GE Younger Writers Award, both in 1987 and 1986, and was nominated for a Pushcart Prize in 1983. In 1984, he was awarded a fellowship to Yaddo, where he completed *FIRE WITHOUT WITNESS*, an epic poem centered on the life of Michelangelo, to be published in the fall of 1988 by British American.

Nepo has taught creative writing at Skidmore College and Empire State College, and currently teaches creative writing and literature at SUNY Albany, where he received his Doctor of Arts degree in 1980.

He lives with his wife, Anne, in East Greenbush, New York.